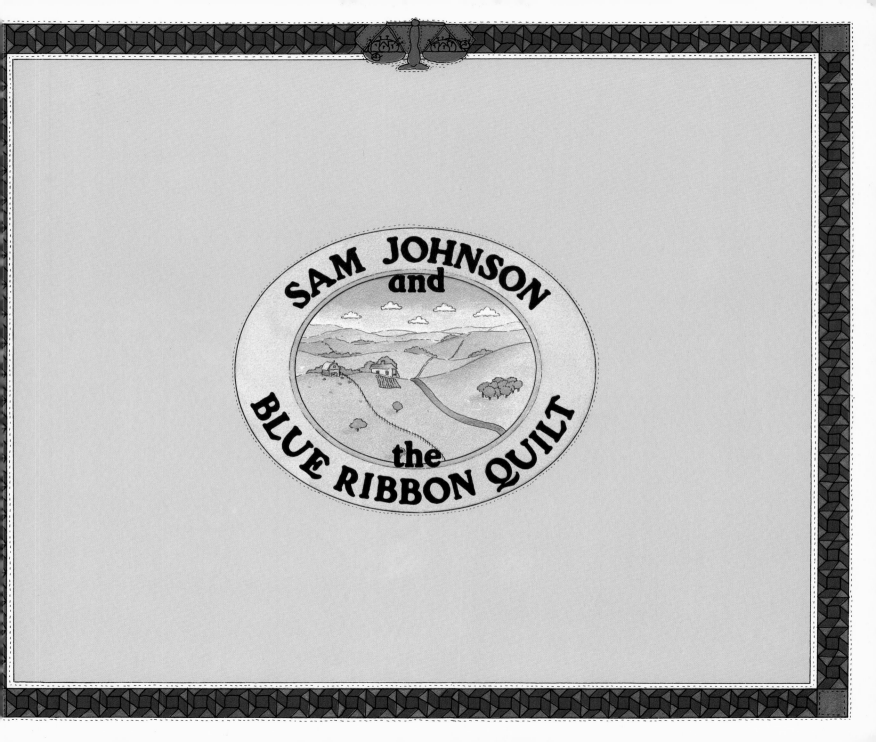

SAM JOHNSON
and
the
BLUE RIBBON QUILT

Library of Congress Cataloging in Publication Data.
Ernst, Lisa Campbell. Sam Johnson and the blue ribbon
quilt. Summary: While mending the awning over the pig
pen, Sam discovers that he enjoys sewing the various
patches together but meets with scorn and ridicule when
he asks his wife if he could join her quilting club.
[1. Quilting—Fiction. 2. Sex role—Fiction] I. Title.
PZ7.E7323Sam 1983 [E] 82-9980 ISBN 0-688-01516-6
ISBN 0-688-01517-4 (lib.bdg.)—0-688-11505-5 (pbk.)

Lothrop, Lee & Shepard Books · New York

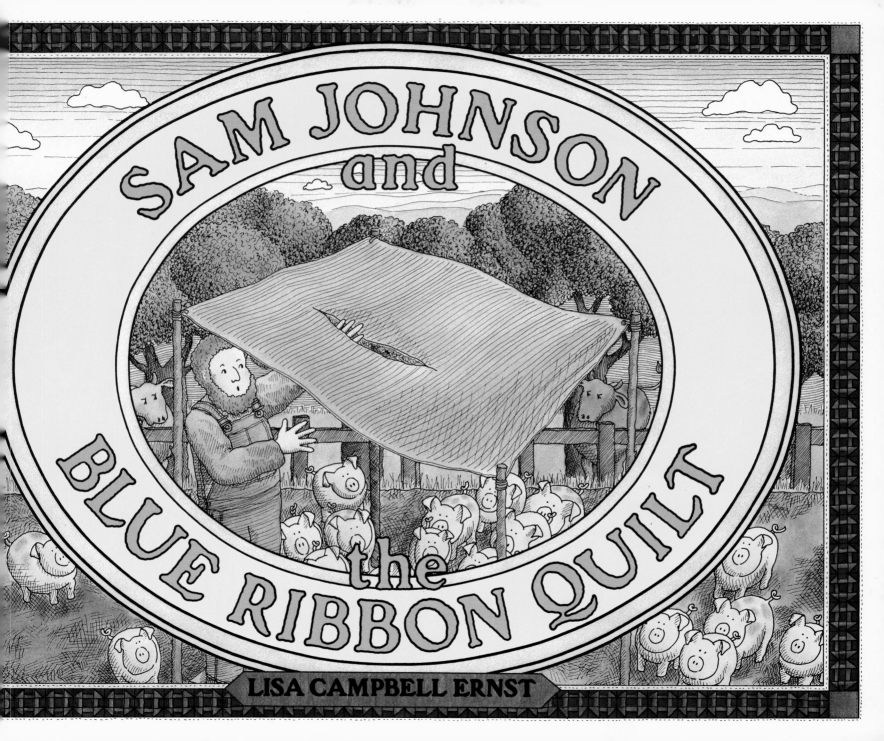

SAM JOHNSON and the BLUE RIBBON QUILT

LISA CAMPBELL ERNST

for Lee

Sam Johnson discovered a torn awning over the pig's pen one morning while his wife was out of town. That evening he settled down to mend the tear himself, taking pieces of cloth from Mrs. Johnson's scrap bag to patch the hole.

At first, just running the needle in and out of the fabric was hard work, but as the evening wore on, Sam became more expert. Soon he was having a fine time choosing patches of different shapes and colors. It was sunrise before he leaned back to admire his night's work.

"What a masterpiece!" he exclaimed, turning the design about. "Just wait until Sarah sees this. She'll be mighty impressed."

By the time Mrs. Johnson returned that afternoon, Sam was waiting for her on the porch.

"That's very nice, dear," she said, giving his handiwork a quick glance. "I'm glad to see you kept yourself busy while I was away."

"But Sarah, don't you think it's beautiful?" Sam protested. When Mrs. Johnson did not answer, Sam went on, "I had so much fun doing it that I've decided to join your quilting club!"

"Now Sam, dear," Mrs. Johnson chuckled nervously. "It's very nice that you enjoyed your little project while I was away. But my quilting club? Don't get carried away. That's no place for a man to be—sewing is women's work."

But Mrs. Johnson wasn't laughing the next night as she and Sam rode together to the weekly meeting of the Rosedale Women's Quilting Club. Nor did she crack a smile when they walked through the meeting-room door and all the ladies turned and stared.

Sam cleared his throat. "Good evening," he said calmly. "I've decided to join your club."

After a few seconds of silence, a small snicker was heard. Then another, and another. Soon everyone in the whole room was laughing. Everyone, that is, but Sam. "Don't be silly," the club president said. "We can't have a man here bungling everything! Our most important quilt of the year is coming up—the one for the county fair contest. Why don't you go join the men's horseshoe or checkers club if you want something to do with your time?"

Sam stalked out of the room.

The next morning his hastily hung posters
were scattered all around the county.

Sam's speech that evening was a rousing one. "Men," he began, "we have a very serious problem on our hands." He described what happened to the awning, waving it high in the air, and then what happened at the quilting club meeting. He talked about freedom and the country and even about the Declaration of Independence. Finally he explained about the quilt contest at the county fair.

"Are you willing," he said, "to prove these ladies wrong?"

The men looked at one another and timidly nodded.

"Are you ready," his voice became louder, "to show you can do more with your hands than plow a field?"

"Yes," answered a small chorus of voices.

"Then I say," he finished, "we should enter that contest ourselves."

This time, everyone clapped and cheered. The Rosedale Men's Quilting Club had officially begun.

The county fair was only a month away, so the men didn't have much time. They met every night in Sam's barn, working—awkwardly at first—on their Flying Geese design.

Meanwhile, the women were hard at work on their Sailboats pattern. In the beginning, they thought the men's club was a joke. "Quilting is much too delicate a job for men," they agreed. Soon, though, there were doubts.

"I wonder what their quilt looks like," the women's club president said one evening. "I wonder what colors they are using." No one spoke up, but a hush fell over the room as everyone stitched faster.

In their final week, each club worked far into the night,

making their stitches small and neat, their seams straight and exact.

At dawn on the day of the contest, the men and the women gently folded their quilts, laid them in the back of their wagons, and set out for the fairground. It was a cool, clear morning following a night of heavy rain. Each group wrapped its entry in old blankets to protect it from lingering drops..

As the wagons passed through the fairground gates, the Rosedale quilting clubs paused a moment and, looking quite smug, nodded their heads in greeting. Just then a huge gust of wind blew up and both quilts were swept into the air. Each landed with a light splat in a giant mud puddle.

No one could believe what had happened.

"All that work," Sam Johnson moaned.

"All those hours and hours. And now, look. Ruined."

But then the women peered at the men's quilt and noticed how beautiful it was, and the men saw for the first time that the women's quilt was quite beautiful too. "You really did a wonderful job," they said to each other. "Too bad neither of us will win."

"Wait!" Sam cried, as everyone headed back to the wagons. "I have an idea."

Dairy Barn ⇦

Exhibition Hall

Livestock ⇨

Show Ring ⇨

All that morning and all that afternoon, the Rosedale Men's Quilting Club and the Rosedale Women's Quilting Club worked together. Carefully, delicately, they cut out the unsoiled sections of each quilt. Then they pieced together the unsplattered fabric. As the sun set, the last stitches were being put in to complete their amazing design.

The fair was a great success. Elijah Pool's hog tipped the scales at a record weight. Harriet Eyman's apple-raisin pie swept every baking prize.

And for the quilting contest, first prize was awarded to the just plain Rosedale Quilting Club.

"What's the name of your unusual design?" Sam Johnson was asked.

He paused for a moment, thinking, then replied. "Why, Flying Sailboats, of course."

The border designs
in this book are actual quilt
patterns, each relating to the content of
its particular picture. Beginning with Open
Book on the opening page, the quilt patterns
illustrated are Hole in the Barn Door, Variable
Star, Rising Sun, Double Wedding Ring, Shoo-
Fly, Trumpet Vine, Bow Tie, Flying Geese,
Sailboat, Spools, Hour Glass, Whirlwind,
Broken Dishes, Friendship Star,
Nelson's Victory, and Tree
Everlasting.